Grace Clarke

A book of rhymes

Grace Clarke

A book of rhymes

ISBN/EAN: 9783337259402

Printed in Europe, USA, Canada, Australia, Japan

Cover: Foto ©Andreas Hilbeck / pixelio.de

More available books at **www.hansebooks.com**

A BOOK

OF

RHYMES

GRACE CLARKE

NEW YORK

MDCCCXCVII

W HAT have we here ; a book of rhymes ?
        I wonder how the book will fare.
Who has not said, a score of times,
" What have we here, a book of rhymes ;
A little peal of tinkling chimes ? "
    (How much these rhymsters make us bear.)
What have we here ; a book of rhymes ?
    I wonder how the book will fare.

CONTENTS

JAPANESE LOVE SONG

A MOON-RAY bright glides from above
    To kiss the peach blossom, his love,
  And sweet from her fragrant lips
                He slips
Into the chamber of my dove.

My sleeping dove, with the almond eyes !
Across her smiling mouth he flies
  Leaving a track of silver there
                To bear
Witness of the captured prize.

Still speeding on, the naughty thief,
To her ear with boldness past belief,
  And murmurs in that pearly shell
                To tell
Of both the kisses, sweet and brief.

Great Buddha ! grant this boon, I pray,
Let me become a bright moon-ray,
  And, mingling with my loved one's dream,
              At gleam
Of dawn, fade from her sight away.

ONLY

IT was only a rose,
  And who would suppose
    That he lived on its perfume for many a day.

It was only a smile,
But its infinite wile
    In her magical manner of giving it, lay.

He was only a boy,
And his heart was a toy
    For her highness to play with, then cast it away.

GRANDMAMA'S GIRLISH GOWNS

PALED and yellowed by time are they—
   Even Love cannot say " Nay."
   Old and faded, once new and gay,
   Bright and gay in a far-off day,
When Grandmama was a girl, they say,
Grandmama now so worn and gray.

Sweet with scents of the damask rose,
Blossom's fashion comes and goes;
   And their perfume, now passé
   Was well liked in a far-off day,
When Grandmama was a girl, they say,
Grandmama now so worn and gray.

On the daintiest of them all,
I see a tear that she let fall.
   Grandpapa kissed the rest away,
   Far away, in a far-off day,
When Grandmama was a girl, they say,
Grandmama now so worn and gray.

But a truce to these musings vain,
In their cedar chest again
   All the dainty gowns I'll lay;
   Memories of a far-off day
When Grandmama was a girl, they say,
Grandmama now so worn and gray.

TO ROBERT HERRICK

SO well he loved the Spring, that when she weaves
  Her misty bud-strewn robe of tender leaves,
No one there is who loves him, but that grieves
                    He is not here to see.

(12)

THE ANGLER

CUPID upon a summer day,
Went a-fishing, so they say.

He wove a net of tender wiles
And baited it with merry smiles.

He caught a rose, he caught a kiss.
" Alas !" cried he, " I something miss !"

And, trembling with a sudden fear,
He dropped into his net a tear.

Then lo ! he found it to contain
The heart that he had longed to gain.

Lovers ! be not too bold and gay,
Sometimes a doubt will win the day.

CONTRADICTION

THE March winds tossed her curls about—
　　She only gave a charming pout;
　　But when, with gentlest touch, I tried
　　The self-same thing, egad, she cried!

The April sunshine kissed her cheek—
She only smiled—she did not speak.
　　But when, made bold by this, I tried
　　The self-same thing, egad, she cried!

And when in May I asked her why
She acted thus in days gone by,
　　She answered, " Sweetheart, don't you know ?
　　It was because I loved you so ! "

THE RHYMSTER

M Y thought exhausts itself in four,
  Or eight lines at the most.
  Hence I affect the " Triolet,"
  The Quatrain and the Toast.

'Tis well to know how far to climb,
How deep to dip one's oars.
  And though you'll ne'er say " Genius rare ! "
  I'll not be classed with " Bores."

CLAIRE

A CLOUD of tulle and gems and flowers
    Whence rose a neck and face so fair,
I wondered if all Beauty's dowers
    Were not enshrined in Claire !

The tiny head so proudly held,
    The tiny foot upon the stair,
My heart with keenest rapture swelled
    To first behold her there.

But afterward ? A sorry Fate !
    To join that ever-crowding throng,
Who, lingering in torment, wait,
    And know 'twill not be long

Before the noble prince appears,
    Wooing, triumphant in his pride ;
When I shall go, half blind with tears,
    To see Claire made his bride.

But 'tis a privilege to break
    One's heart for her. Perfection's rare !
So, go my little song, and take
    Another heart to Claire.

CAPRICE

WITH humbly folded hands,
　　The tiny Phyllis stands,
And holds her cheek to let me kiss;
I gently take my fill, for this
Is sure a very kindly miss
　　Of six!

With humbly folded hands
I kneel while Phyllis stands;
I would not dare to beg one kiss,
For though to you, strange seemeth this,
I love her more than that kind miss
　　Of six.

AQUATIC COURTSHIP

"WE pull together well," he cried.
    " Yes, Jack, we do," she softly sighed.
" Would you agree to face life's tide
With me forever at your side? "
" If I might steer," she quick replied.

ST. AUGUSTINE

WHERE was Phyllis all the while
  That the stormy March winds blew ?
Free her tender heart from guile,
  Honest, brave, and true.

But she parries, with a smile,
  This my query—blushing too—
" Oh, 'twas many a weary mile,
  Far from town—and you ! "

Harder pressed, if know I must,
  Many wonders she had seen,
Kneeling awestruck in the dust,
  To St. Augustine !

Phyllis, this will never do ;
  If you've kept the Lenten time
Worshipping a saint or two
  In a southern clime,

It is nothing to conceal
  Or to cause that rosy hue
O'er your blushing face to steal,
  Fill your eyes with dew.

Was the saint made manifest ?
  Did you walk with him, perchance ?
Did he wait on your behest,
  Hang upon your glance ?

And when sunset's golden rose
  Faded from the fairy scene,
Did you feel your heart unclose
  To St. Augustine ?

Well, I wish him joy.   I may ?
  Oh, I knew it ! truly blessed
Was the saint to whom, that day,
  Phyllis stood confessed.

For your romance, sweet and fair,
  Lovelier setting could not be ;
May your saint his halo wear ;
  Would that I were he.

TWO SONGS

A BIRD sang on a hawthorn tree,
    " Te weet! Te weet! Te weet! "
And one who listened said, in glee,
    " He sings that life is sweet! "
Another groaned, " He cries to me,
    ' Defeat! Defeat! Defeat! ' "
But still the bird sang on the tree,
    " Te weet! Te weet! Te weet! "

IN SLIPPERS SMALL

A VILLANELLE

IN slippers small, of satin, glistening white,
  My lady knelt before the altar rail.
And promised unto me her solemn plight.

Her charming face was blanched, but not with
    fright.
  A loving bride does not her fate bewail,
In slippers small, of satin, glistening white.

What fact should cause her other than delight,
  As she was wed, by words that could not fail,
And promised unto me her solemn plight ?

I wondered as I watched her all bedight
  With fragrant purity, why she grew pale,
In slippers small, of satin, glistening white.

To me the whole world looked at once more bright
  When she was made my wife, so fair and frail,
And promised unto me her solemn plight.

But quick I heard, " My dainty shoes are tight,"
  And knew why still she trembled 'neath her veil
In slippers *small*, of satin, glistening white,
  And promised unto me her solemn plight.

WHERE THE CLOVER BLOSSOMS BLOW

A SONG

WHERE the clover blossoms blow,
   Crimson-tipped, and white as snow,
Stood a laughing maid.

Where the clover blossoms blow,
Pouting lips said, " Go ! Go ! Go ! "
   And I went, dismayed.

Where the clover blossoms blow,
Turned for one last look and, lo !
   Saw, though half afraid,

Where the clover blossoms blow,
Trembling hands which beckoned, so
   I went back—and stayed !

(23)

EFFORT

A THOUSAND tiny billows shine,
   Flecked with froth of bubbling brine ;
A thousand tiny billows break
Before the perfect wave shall wake.

ARTLESS ART

THEY say, to write a triolet,
   One must be very wise;
Well versed in rules that chafe and fret,
  They say, to write a triolet.
  I strive not for such skill, and yet,
I almost hold the prize,
  They say to write a triolet
One must be *very* wise.

THE BRIDE OF THE CHINESE PRINCE

A RONDEL

SUCH a prim little bride for the Emperor's heir;
    She couldn't have been much over four.
But solemnly sat on the inlaid floor,
Like a carven figure of ivory ware.

And I sadly mused " What is held in store
For that tiny maiden, joy or care ?"
Such a prim little bride for the Emperor's heir;
She couldn't have been much over four.

There were golden arrows in her hair,
Twisted and coiled a la Pompadour;
Her blue silk robe was 'broidered o'er
With fiery dragons and blossoms rare.
Such a prim little bride for the Emperor's heir
She couldn't have been much over four.

PEGASUS IN HARNESS

M Y Pegasus was wont to soar
    In very lofty flights of rhyme.
With him I hoped to reach Fame's door,
       Some time

I met a. jolly girl—Ah, me !
    She likes this more than " dainty maid,"
And all her whimsies now must be
       Obeyed.

I felt 'twas love with me at sight,
    And in an ode told all my joy,
Sending it to her that same night
       By boy.

'Twas my last ode ; the answer came,
    Making a Paradise of Earth !
But she treated those lines, so full of flame,
       With mirth !

She said, " Dear Jack, it's yes ; but, dear,
    I like you best to talk in prose,
Though to anything, I'd say, I fear,
       It goes.

" I do not mind a joking verse,
    But nothing that's at all high-flown.
It always makes my temper worse,
       Your own."

So now, my Pegasus, must jig
    And gambol like a circus horse,
And I—why I don't care a fig—
            Of course.

What do I want of laurel wreaths?
    Why should I wish and strive for fame?
'Tis my greatest honor when she breathes
            My name!

A POET

I USED to be an honest man,
  Before I took to rhyme ;
But the wide poetic license
  Will enlarge one's views—in time.
I used to think I would not part
  With truth for any pelf,
But now the lyre of which I sing
  Is, frequently, myself !

For instance this I write : " Oh, Love,
  I would that thou wert here,
To lay thy cool hand on my brow
  And wipe away grief's tear."
Now what sheer nonsense all that is ;
  Great heavens ! as if I
Would let my love, who worships me,
  Behold her hero *cry!*

And then again I pen these lines :
  " A crust of bread and fame
Are more than if I feasted well,
  With an unnoted name."
Mere fallacies ; Fame in these days
  Is not content with bread,
And where's the hungry bard who'd not
  · Prefer a feast instead ?

(29)

Of course I'd rather stick to truth,
  Were truth and verse not foes ;
So what we poets really think
  The public seldom knows.
But when my purse is very plump,
  The public on its knees,
To crown me lion of an hour,
  I'll say just what I please !

MY LADY'S FAN

RONDEAU

MY lady's fan waves to and fro,
  And with its perfumed breath doth blow,
All painful doubtings from my mind,
For I can feel her smile is kind,
The gracious motion is so slow!
'Twas but a little while ago
(And for what cause I do not know)
  A frowning face was hid behind
    My lady's fan.

I hear a sob—adagio—
And haste to soothe my lady's woe ;
  I thank thee, little boy-god, blind,
  That I such tender welcome find,
Behind that yielding portico,
    My lady's fan !

(31)

AN IMPERFECT NOTE

DOROTHY wrote on a scented sheet,
   With a golden pen, tipped bright with pearl,
And her writing was extremely neat
   For a nineteenth century girl.

Her choice of language was clear as day,
   And her punctuation bold and black;
" Now, what," I think I hear you say,
   " Did Dorothy's missive lack ? "

Dorothy knew, when she penned that note,
   That one tiny word was lacking there,
And, as a substitute, she wrote
   A word, for which I don't care.

I'll tell you, perhaps you'll guess
   The curious truth—to me 'twas so—
That the word I wished to see was " Yes,"
   And the word I saw was " No ! "

A SPANISH IDYL

L UISITA, Luisita,
   When I went at dusk to meet her,
Laid in my hand a rosebud and on my lips a
   kiss ;

The rose was very sweet, and yet, its perfume
   seemed amiss,
For the kiss was far, far sweeter,
Luisita ! Luisita !

ST. CUPID

L OVE wore a very reverent guise,
But there was mischief in his eyes.

He donned the surplice and the bands,
But there were roses in his hands.

Said I, " 'Tis Goodness, Saints above !
And yet how much he looks like Love."

(34)

WHAT'S IN A NAME?

I LOVED a girl; a lovely girl,
   Like Herrick's damsel; fair was she
With ruby lips and " teeth of pearl,"
   Well worthy of my minstrelsy.
And here I note, lest you forget,
   My name is William, some say " Bill."
Great Shakespeare bore the same, and yet,
   Only to hear it makes me ill.

Ah ! ever since one fateful day
   Its noble charms began to pall,
When, armed with a huge bouquet,
   I stood and trembled in her hall.
I had resolved to test my fate,
   And what 'twould be I could not guess,
But somehow I had thought, of late,
   That she perhaps would tell me " Yes."

A sound of weeping caught my ear,
   I knew it was my darling's sob,
And, though it made me pale to hear,
   I stayed my hand upon the knob.
Ye Gods ! My throbbing heart stood still,
   For this she said, without a doubt,
" I know that I have lost my Bill,
   The Bill I cannot do without ! "

Enough! I rushed unto her side,
    Crying, "Look up! Oh, maiden sweet,
I still am yours" (with lover's pride).
    "Behold, your Bill is at your feet!"
With eyes amazed she viewed me o'er,
    "It's a five dollar note! and please,"
Said she, "It isn't on the floor.
    You'd better get up off your knees."

THE ADVOCATE

IN cap and gown, Love pleads unto me,
　That I may alter the degree,
　　Which sentences an erring knight,
　　To go forever from my sight ;
It seems he would a prisoner be.

Love pleads, " Thou must not set him free,
For he well likes captivity."
　　I' faith, Love proves him most contrite,
　　　　In cap and gown.

" Sir Knight, when on thy bended knee,
　Thou provest I am dear to thee,
　　I'd feared another story, quite,
　　And so, my haughty words despite,
Thank Love, for he has won the plea,"
　　　　In cap and gown.

TO F. E. C.

A TRIOLET

LIKE birds that gently light and fly,
　　Each breathing forth a joyous song,
Her numbered years are flitting by,
Like birds that gently light and fly.
Unto the higher, brighter sky
　　They wing their peaceful way along,
Like birds that gently light and fly,
　　Each breathing forth a joyous song.

THE FAIR BLOSSOM

SHE loved them all so well
　　She could not tell
　　Which flower she thought most fair.
" The Lily and the Rose
Such sweets disclose,
　　To choose I do not dare."

The violet's purple bloom
And faint perfume
　　Held her within their thrall.
" Which one, of all that blow,
I do not know,
　　Woe's me ! I love them all."

She looked into the glass,
She saw a lass
　　Most pleasing to the view ;
" And who is this fair maid ? "
I am afraid
　　The fairest flower she knew.

For neck and brow were white
As lilies, quite,
　　Her cheeks rose pinks and reds,
And from her mouth, red-lipped,
Such fragrance slipped,
　　The violets hung their heads.

(39)

THE LITTLE RHYMSTER

IT was the little rhymster's boast,
   A solitude he fain would seek,
An eyre on some rock-bound coast,
   To hear the mighty billows speak
The thundrous story; " Then," said he,
   " My pen should chronicle a mind
As wild and stormy as the sea,
   Free and tempestuous as the wind ! "

But lest this happy dream should ne'er
   Be realized, he wrote each week
Lines to fair " Julia's Lock of Hair.
   Her dainty glove and peachy cheek; "
And at the yearly holidays
   The saddened critics always found
A tiny volume of his lays
   In white and gold, octavo, bound.

A RECOLLECTION

SHE was the very fairest maid
   That e'er mine eyes had chanced to see
               (I had not then seen much),
And at the organ sat and played
   Mendelssohn's Wedding March to me
             (She had a lovely touch).
It was a sweet, suggestive air.
   The village church, save just we two
            (The maiden fair and me),
Was quite deserted; she was fair,
   And I, well, what was I to do ?
            (Just wait and you will see)
I did it ! Now, perhaps, you'll guess
   " Undoubtedly he begged a kiss
            (Perhaps for three or four)
And asked the maid his life to bless,
   To make it one long dream of bliss"
            (A paradise and more).
All wrong; for this was years ago,
   And I had broken some small rule
            My teacher disobeyed,
And, for a penalty, must blow
   The organ bellows, after school
            While teacher sang and played.

TO PHYLLIS

(whom I won, by feigning friendship)

CUPID played at dominoes
   He laid no counters out in rows,
Yet won the game.   In such a way
He tries to win one, every day.
He wore a mask of deepest black,
A hooded cloak upon his back,
   And when my Phyllis passed that way,
   He cried, " I'm Friendship, prithee stay,

" Stay, and fold me to thy breast."
Cupid, it was a cruel jest,
   That when, within her tender arms,
   (As Friendship causing no alarms)
You plunged your feathered shaft so deep
She ne'er can lull the pain to sleep.
   A cruel jest, but ah, how sweet,
   That I, once captive at her feet,
Her willing slave, am, by your art,
Made king and master of her heart !

AURORA

HER airy robe, half mist, half light,
    Is jeweled o'er with rainbow dew ;
  Her eyes reflect the midnight's blue,
Her locks the sun-ray's bright.

She lingers, watching as she stands,
    Diana in her silver boat,
  Across the cloud-waves, fading, float,
Waving her pallid hands.

Then turns, a rose glow on her face,
    To feel Apollo's burning kiss,
  But one brief moment's perfect bliss,
Then he, too, vanishes through space.

ONE SUMMER DAY

I KNELT by Phyllis while she played
  On such a summer day as this ;
An hour we lingered in the shade—
  How music doth our cares dismiss !

While o'er the strings her fingers strayed
  Who broke the chord once with a kiss ?
I knelt by Phyllis while she played
  On such a summer day as this.

Though ne'er again " Loves Serenade "
  Shall sound within my heart's abyss,
And Hope is dead, with Youth's brief bliss ;
  I knelt by Phyllis while she played
On such a summer day as this.

THE CHOICE OF PHYLLIS LEE

" IF all my lovers in a row,
    Held out their arms to me,
Ah ! which to choose I well should know,"
    Said bonny Phyllis Lee.

" If Roger, with the bold, black eyes,
    Fell on his bended knee,
I'd answer, spite of all his cries,
    ' Nay, lad, I'm not for thee.'

" And Jack or Hal their cause might plead,
    But neither's could I be ;
These youths are goodly youths, indeed,
    But still—I'm Phyllis Lee.

" 'Tis one who ne'er hath talked of love,
    Who from my thrall seems free,
Who holds his head so high above
    My own, he does not see

" That for him, in a sweet accord
    My heart throbs ecstasy,
I fain would greet *him* as my lord,"
    Said bonny Phyllis Lee.

LOVE'S ROSE

HE watched the rose of Love unfold
    Its crimson petals 'neath his gaze,
Until he saw the heart of gold
Which could illume Life's maze.

He felt like kneeling to this flower,
    " Too pure, too sweet it is for me ! "
But still it made a happy hour
    To linger near and see

How soft two bright eyes were for him :
    How quickly beat a girlish heart ;
Alas ! to make those eyes grow dim
    'Twould be a coward's part !

But, tempted sore, he plucked the rose
    And bound it on his manly brow,
Where still it breathes perfume, and glows
    No fairer then than now.

JEFFERSON AT MONTICELLO

BENEATH the window, from whence he beheld
 The fairest vista in Virginia fair,
 A rose-tree trembles in the summer air,
And all the sense of happiness that welled
 Within that manly heart, I strangely share
Illusion which I would not have dispelled.

Again with Jefferson I sit at ease
 And watch the sunlit valley from the hill;
I hear the murmuring wind sigh through the trees;
 "Friend, though this man wrought deeds both good
   and ill,
 Amidst his virtues 'twas a gracious will
That placed such beauty where it most could please."

ERRATA

On page 37, first line, for " unto "
　　read " with."

On page 40, third line, for " eyre "
　　read " eyrie."